Fables

retold by Emily Kavicky
illustrated by Dani Jones

 Harcourt

SCHOOL PUBLISHERS

Requests for permission to make copies of any part of the work should be addressed to School Permissions and Copyrights, Harcourt, Inc., 6277 Sea Harbor Drive, Orlando, Florida 32887-6777. Fax: 407-345-2418.

HARCOURT and the Harcourt Logo are trademarks of Harcourt, Inc., registered in the United States of America and/or other jurisdictions.

Printed in China

ISBN 10: 0-15-350496-X
ISBN 13: 978-0-15-350496-9

Ordering Options
ISBN 10: 0-15-350333-5 (Grade 3 Below-Level Collection)
ISBN 13: 978-0-15-350333-7 (Grade 3 Below-Level Collection)
ISBN 10: 0-15-357483-6 (package of 5)
ISBN 13: 978-0-15-357483-2 (package of 5)

11 12 13 14 15 0940 12 11 10

The Lion and the Mouse

One day, a little mouse was skipping through a vast jungle. The mouse did not realize that an enormous lion was sleeping nearby. As the mouse skipped by, the lion reached out and caught the little mouse.

"I am going to eat you, little mouse,"
exclaimed the lion.

"Oh, please don't eat me," begged
the little mouse.

The lion decided that the mouse
wasn't big enough to make a good
meal. He let the mouse go.

A few days later, the little mouse
overheard a great roar and discovered
the lion caught in some ropes.

"I have been caught by a hunter. Please help me!" cried the lion.

The little mouse said, "You set me free, so I will help you." The little mouse jumped on top of the lion and chewed apart the ropes. The ropes fell away, and the lion was free.

The lion shook off the ropes and grabbed the little mouse. For a moment, the mouse was afraid, but the grateful lion hugged the mouse in his big paws.

From that day on, the lion and the mouse were best friends. The lion learned that it does not matter how big or small your friends are. It matters how good a friend they are!

The Hare and the Tortoise

One day, Mr. Hare, who was very vain, was boasting about how fast he could run.

"I dare any animal to run a race against me!" declared the hare.

A tortoise slowly moved to the front of the crowd. "I will gladly race against you," suggested Mr. Tortoise.

The hare said, "What a foolish tortoise. You have good intentions, but you will never win!"

"You boast a lot," replied the tortoise, "but we'll see who wins this race."

All the forest animals lined up to watch the race. Mr. Hare and Mr. Tortoise were ready, so Mr. Fox raised his arm and shouted, "On your mark, get set, GO!"

Off ran the hare, leaving the tortoise
moving slowly along behind him. The
hare was so swift that he was sure he
would win. "How could a slowpoke
tortoise beat me?" he thought. "I think
I'll take a nap!" Mr. Hare settled under
a tree and promptly fell asleep.

Meanwhile, the tortoise kept going
at a slow but steady pace.

As the tortoise crept along, he passed the sleeping hare. Finally, the hare woke up, stretched, and ran off to finish the race. To his surprise, the tortoise was ahead of him!

As the tortoise crossed the finish line, he thought, "Slow and steady wins the race."

The hare crept away as the forest animals cheered wildly for the winner.

City Mouse and Country Mouse

One day, City Mouse went to visit her cousin, Country Mouse. As City Mouse came to the door, Country Mouse hugged her. "Come in, cousin. I only have bread, beans, bacon, and cheese, but everything I have is yours to share," said Country Mouse. City Mouse sat down to eat the simple food.

City Mouse said, "Cousin, I cannot understand how you can eat such simple food. You must come to the city, and I will show you how to live!"

The next day, City Mouse and Country Mouse left for the big city. When they arrived at City Mouse's house, the mice entered the grand dining room. Country Mouse had never seen such fine food!

As the mice began to eat, Country Mouse knocked over a fork. The sound woke the family dog, and the mice heard barking and growling!

"What is that?" cried Country Mouse.

"It's just the family dog," replied City Mouse.

"I don't think I like having a dog so close!" said Country Mouse, as the dog ran into the dining room. "Good-bye, cousin. I am going back to the country immediately!"

"Good-bye cousin," said City Mouse.

"I would rather eat simple foods in peace than fancy foods in fear," Country Mouse thought as she hurried out the door.

Think Critically

1. What was the author trying to say in the story of the lion and the mouse?

2. How are City Mouse and Country Mouse different?

3. In "The Hare and the Tortoise," what lesson did you learn?

4. What did the hare do that allowed the tortoise to win the race?

5. Which fable was your favorite? Why?

 **Social Studies**

City and Country City Mouse and Country Mouse lived in very different places. Do you live in the city or the country? Make a list of some of the differences that you think there would be if you lived in the other place.

School-Home Connection Tell one of the fables in this book in your own words to a friend or family member. Then talk about the moral of the story and what it means to you.